THE GRIEFER'S REVENGE

THE GRIEFER'S REVENGE

AN UNOFFICIAL LEAGUE OF GRIEFERS ADVENTURE, #3

Winter Morgan

Sky Pony Press
New York

Copyright © 2015 by Hollan Publishing, Inc.

Minecraft® is a registered trademark of Notch Development AB

The Minecraft game is copyright © Mojang AB

Sky Pony Press books may be purchased in bulk at special discounts for sales promotion, corporate gifts, fund-raising, or educational purposes. Special editions can also be created to specifications. For details, contact the Special Sales Department, Sky Pony Press, 307 West 36th Street, 11th Floor, New York, NY 10018 or info@skyhorsepublishing.com.

Sky Pony® is a registered trademark of Skyhorse Publishing, Inc.®, a Delaware corporation.

Minecraft® is a registered trademark of Notch Development AB.
The Minecraft game is copyright © Mojang AB.

Visit our website at www.skyponypress.com.

10 9 8 7 6 5 4 3 2 1

Library of Congress Cataloging-in-Publication Data is available on file.

Cover photo by Megan Miller

Print ISBN: 978-1-63450-597-0
Ebook ISBN: 978-1-63450-598-7

Printed in Canada

TABLE OF CONTENTS

1
CHOSEN

A man and woman wearing matching red jackets approached Violet as she placed the final wooden plank on a small house she was building.

"Are you Violet?" asked the woman.

"Yes," Violet answered. She immediately noticed the official-looking patches on both of their jackets and wondered what they wanted from her. "Why do you ask?"

"We've heard you are the best builder in the Overworld," stated the man in the red jacket.

Violet blushed. She disliked attention and simply loved building. "Thanks," she replied.

Violet saw her friend Noah approaching. "I see they found you," he called out.

Noah stood next to Violet as the woman in the red jacket spoke: "We are from the Minecraft Olympic Committee. Your town was chosen to host the Olympic games, and we want you to build the stadiums for the games."

"Stadiums?" Violet questioned. She couldn't imagine how many stadiums they wanted her to build.

The man answered, "We need you to build four stadiums. People will be traveling from all around the Overworld both to participate and to watch these games. The construction is a very high profile job. Many people will see your work."

Violet was excited, but also a bit nervous. She had never worked on a project that was this important. She worried they might not like the stadiums she would build. "Four? Are there specific designs that I have to use?"

"The Minecraft Olympics will consist of four major events. We will need a stadium for each event," the woman replied.

The man in the red jacket clarified, "The first game is a player versus player game. This means you need to construct a stadium where two players can battle. That stadium also needs a small room with two beds where the players can respawn."

Many building ideas swirled through Violet's head and she answered enthusiastically, "I think I can do that. It sounds like fun!"

"The other three games involve different stadiums. We need one for a sprinting competition. So you'll need to construct a track," the woman in the red jacket explained, and she went into various details about the stadium.

The man told Violet about the final two Olympic games and their specialized stadiums. "One of the major events that will attract the most attention is the Battle of the Mobs. You'll need to create various mob spawners and a stage where skilled players show off their skills by battling hostile mobs."

Violet had never created a mob spawner—that was something Daniel and his evil rainbow griefer army were experts at crafting. Violet thought about Daniel and how he might affect the Olympic games. The town hadn't heard from Daniel since they convinced his rainbow griefer army to change skins and live peacefully in their town. She wondered if he knew the town was hosting the Olympics, and whether he might cause trouble. But she knew she couldn't get distracted. She had to focus on her job. She had just been asked to build Olympic stadiums! This was a dream come true.

"I'll admit, I have never built a mob spawner before, but I have great plans for the stage and the stadium. And I'm sure I can find someone to assist me in crafting the mob spawners," replied Violet.

"You can hire assistants for the project. It's a very large building job and you'll need lots of help," added the woman.

"The final stadium is for our archery competition," the man explained to Violet.

Noah asked, "Do you use commands in the archery competition?"

"Yes," the man replied, "if you hit the bull's-eye, a redstone lamp lights up."

"These games sound incredible," remarked Noah. "Can anybody participate, or do you have to be invited?"

The man addressed Noah, "We have singled out the strongest players in the Overworld. But we will also host local tryouts for people in your town who might want to participate, too."

"I'd love to try out!" Noah couldn't contain his excitement.

Violet was surprised. She didn't think Noah was very competitive, but he was a skilled fighter and sprinter and would definitely make it into one of the games.

"I just realized we never introduced ourselves," the woman in the red jacket laughed. "We were so excited about asking you to build the stadiums that we forgot our manners. I'm Nina."

"I'm Mac. We're from the Minecraft Olympic Committee, as we said." The man in the red jacket smiled at Violet and Noah. "And we're very excited to have you build these stadiums. I think the Olympic games are going to be great fun. You have such a peaceful, scenic village; it's the perfect spot for the games."

Kaboom! An explosion was heard in the distance.

"What was that?" Violet looked for smoke.

"I'm not sure. It doesn't sound like a creeper." Noah was nervous. He hoped it wasn't Daniel.

Violet noticed her friend Angela running toward them. "Someone blew up my farm with blocks of TNT!" she called to her friends.

Violet introduced Angela to Nina and Mac, explaining that the Minecraft Olympics were to be held in their town.

Mac interrupted, "We thought this was a peaceful town . . . that it was free of griefers."

Nina frowned and said, "I think we may have to consider another town."

"Oh no!" Violet blurted out. She had just been offered the best job of her life and now it might be taken away. The Olympic games would also be great for their town. They would bring a lot of business to the small village shops and increase their opportunity for trading.

"We will figure out who blew up our friend Angela's farm and will make sure the town is ready for the Olympics," Noah said confidently.

"Yes, we have fought griefers in the past and won. We can do it again," added Violet.

"I'm sure that's the case," Mac said, but Nina interrupted him.

"We need to discuss this, Mac. If you could please excuse us for a moment," Nina said as she glanced at Violet.

Violet saw them talking together quietly. She worried the games now wouldn't be held in the town because of the destruction of Angela's farm. And she hoped Daniel wasn't behind the explosion. If it was just a random griefer in the town, the battle might be won easily, but Daniel was a sophisticated criminal mastermind. He could devastate the games.

After a few minutes, Nina and Mac stopped talking. They walked toward Violet. Her heart was racing as she eagerly awaited their decision.

2
EXPLOSIONS

"**W**e have decided to go ahead and hold the Olympic games in your village. But you must promise us that you can keep the town secure from griefers and explosions," Nina told Violet.

"Yes, we will do that. And now I will begin building your stadiums," Violet promised the duo from the Minecraft Olympic Committee.

Mac spoke up. "We will drop off the supplies for building the stadiums tomorrow. We need to head back to the Olympic headquarters before dark tonight."

Nina and Mac left the town as the sun began to set. Violet touched Angela on the arm and offered, "You can stay with us at the treehouse tonight."

"Thanks," Angela replied. She was grateful for her good friends, but she was also upset because someone had targeted her farm.

"We'll find out who destroyed your farm in the morning," Noah reassured Angela.

Night had set in. Noah and Violet were about to climb the ladder when Angela cried out, "Ouch!"

"Angela's been hit by an arrow!" Noah shouted as a band of skeletons shot arrows at the trio.

Noah took out his bow and arrow and fired back at the skeletons, striking one and destroying it. Violet grabbed her diamond sword and struck the skeleton that stood behind Angela.

Angela joined Violet in battle, and also struck the skeleton with her diamond sword, destroying the bony beast.

Noah put his bow and arrow back in his inventory and rushed toward the skeletons with his diamond sword. He didn't see the creeper that silently crept up behind him.

"Watch out!" Violet screamed, but it was too late.

Kaboom!

Noah was destroyed by the creeper's self-destructive explosion.

Kaboom!

Another explosion echoed from a distance.

"That doesn't sound like a creeper!" Violet called to Angela as the two attempted to fight off the group of skeletons that surrounded them.

Noah respawned in his bed, and swiftly made it down the ladder from the tree house, shooting arrows at the skeletons.

Violet and Angela lunged at the bony skeletons. *Click. Clack. Clang.* They struck the hostile mobs with their enchanted diamond swords and destroyed the rest of the group.

"Let's go back to the tree house and get some rest," Noah suggested.

"There was an explosion while you were respawning. We have to go find out where it came from," Violet said as she looked off in the distance, trying to figure out what had exploded.

"In the middle of the night? Can't we wait until morning? Trying to find a griefer in the dark is a complete death trap," Noah warned, and he headed for the ladder. "I don't think we're going to solve any mysteries now. We need to sleep."

"Noah, I can't sleep knowing there is trouble brewing in this town. I want the Olympic games to be held here. I promised Nina and Mac this town would be secure," Violet defended her plan.

"But Violet, I think we'll have a better chance of finding the culprit in the daylight," pleaded a weary Noah.

"Noah has a point," Angela said to Violet. "We might encounter zombies, Endermen, and many other hostile mobs on our journey to find out what exploded. By the time we reach the potential griefer, we'll have no energy to fight them. We need to do it in the morning."

Violet was outnumbered. She reluctantly climbed the ladder, pausing when she reached the middle to look out at the town. She eyed the dark landscape for smoke and signs of griefers. There was nothing, until she heard a shout.

"Violet, help!" Ben called out.

He hurried up the ladder. "Someone blew up my house. Luckily, I heard a noise outside and went out to investigate so I wasn't in the house when it exploded."

Ben, Violet, Angela, and Noah sat in the living room of the tree house. "Your house was destroyed?" Violet questioned.

"Yes, somebody blew it up with TNT," Ben said. He was very upset.

"The same thing happened to my farm. Someone blew it up today," Angela told Ben.

"Why did someone destroy our homes?" Ben wondered as he looked out the large window of the tree house.

"I think I know who it is," Violet mused, with a pensive expression.

"Who?" Ben and Angela asked in unison.

Noah also suspected someone. "I think I know who you're talking about, Violet."

"I think it's someone who wants revenge on us for destroying his rainbow griefer army," Violet said as she paced nervously.

"That's who I thought it was, too," Noah admitted. He stood next to Violet.

"Daniel!" Ben and Angela uttered his name in horror.

"Yes," Violet agreed, and she walked to the window. "I don't feel safe here. We might be next on his list. He seems to have targeted all the people who were involved in the attack."

"Not everyone," added Ben, "we weren't the only ones who were battling him."

Suddenly, they heard a noise coming from outside.

"Oh no! I bet Daniel is about to blow this place up!" Violet shouted and dashed toward the ladder.

As they reached the ladder, they saw Hannah and Jack approaching.

"We thought you were Daniel," said Violet in relief.

"Have you seen Daniel?" Jack's voice was shaky. He was terrified.

Hannah and Jack stood in the living room; they were both visibly upset.

"Our homes were destroyed," Hannah told them.

"We didn't hear any explosions," Noah said, with a puzzled look.

"Our homes were flooded with lava," Jack informed them. "But have you seen Daniel?"

"No, but I'm pretty sure this is his work." Violet paced the length of her living room. She knew her house must be next on Daniel's list. She also knew they needed to get some sleep. If they all slept in the tree house, and if it wasn't destroyed, they would all respawn in this same location if something happened to them later on, which would be vital in their fight against Daniel.

Violet calmly directed the group, "We have to go to bed."

"Now?" Hannah was shocked. She was ready to battle Daniel.

"But the house could explode while we're asleep!" Angela was worried.

"It's a chance we'll have to take. If it doesn't explode and we sleep here, we will all respawn in the same place." Violet looked at her friends.

They each walked silently to their beds. Violet pulled the covers over her and hoped that she would awake in the morning. She didn't want the house to explode. Violet closed her eyes and drifted off to sleep.

3
TOO GOOD TO BE TRUE

The sun shone through the large window of the tree house. Violet jumped out of bed. "Wow, the tree house didn't explode!"

"I know. But it's a time bomb," Noah said, as he led the group into the kitchen and offered his guests some cake. "It's just a matter of time before Daniel strikes the house."

"We need to find Daniel," Violet declared before she swallowed a bite of cake. "If we don't, he'll destroy the tree house and stop the Olympic games."

"Where do we start?" asked Hannah.

"We have to suit up and grab our most powerful weapons. Then we have to stick together as we explore the town," instructed Noah.

The gang made their way down the ladder and into town. They walked through the village streets searching for any clues. Valentino the Butcher came out of his shop. "I heard some explosions yesterday. Is that evil griefer back?"

"We're searching for him. We need to make sure this town is secure before we start preparing for the Olympics," Violet told him.

"The Olympics? Are they coming to our town? How wonderful!" Valentino was excited.

The gang continued searching for any rainbow griefers that might be working for Daniel.

"I don't see anything," Jack said, as they checked every street in town.

The gang agreed. There wasn't anything suspicious. They made their way back to the village as Nina and Mac approached them. A group trailed behind the pair, carrying supplies for the stadium.

Nina asked, "Is the town secure?"

Mac questioned further, "Have there been any more explosions?"

Violet stuttered, afraid her response might be the end of the Olympics. She looked at the many people carrying the supplies for the stadiums. She thought of people filling the seats in the stadium, gleefully watching the Olympic games in her town. She wanted to tell Nina and Mac that the town was secure, but she would be lying.

"There was one more explosion and two homes were flooded with lava," confessed Violet. "But I think those were isolated attacks. Someone who wants revenge. I'm not sure they will destroy the games. In fact, I doubt they have that much power."

"Another explosion? And homes flooded with lava? The person behind these attacks seems to have a lot of resources. How can you be so sure they won't attack the games?" Nina questioned Violet.

"I'm sorry, the truth is I'm not sure they won't try to destroy the games. But we promise to work as hard as we can to stop them," replied Violet.

"I'm not sure that's good enough," Mac said as he signaled to the people carrying the supplies to stop.

"I wish you'd reconsider. I think giving up the games because we are threatened by Daniel, an evil griefer, would be a complete shame. I don't want to give him that much power. He doesn't deserve it. And this town doesn't deserve to lose the opportunity to host the games because of him. It's just not fair," pleaded Violet.

"Did you say Daniel?" asked Nina.

"Yes," replied Violet.

"Is this the same Daniel that led a rainbow army in an attempt to take over the Overworld?" questioned Mac.

"Yes," said Noah. "He is the one and only evil head of the rainbow griefer army. But we were able to disband the army, so I think we can avoid an attack at the Olympics. Please don't take this chance away from us."

"We've dealt with Daniel before. He is extremely evil. But you're right—we can't let him stop the Olympics. We will bring some of our own people to help secure the Olympics too. The games will go on!"

Violet and her friends cheered. She felt it was too good to be true. She was getting to build a bunch of stadiums and her town was going to host the Minecraft Olympics.

"While you begin building in the field outside of town, we will start organizing our tryouts for the locals," Mac informed them.

"And we almost forgot," added Nina. "We need you to build a hotel for visitors and housing for the athletes."

"I can do it!" Violet was excited and she gathered all of her good friends to help her build Olympic Village.

The supplies were stacked outside of town. Violet and her friends walked toward the supplies, and she began to give detailed instructions on how they could help her craft the Olympic village. Violet noticed Noah walking away from the construction site.

"Noah," Violet called out. "Where are you going?"

"I am going to help you build the village, but first I'm going to try out for the Olympics," replied Noah.

"What game will you try out for?" Violet asked, as she held a wooden plank in her hand. She had no time to waste; there was a lot of work to be done.

"The Battle of the Mobs," said Noah.

As Noah spoke those words, the sky grew dark and cloudy. Rain began to fall on the town and the construction site. A group of zombies lumbered toward Violet and her friends. Noah didn't have to try out—he was now in the thick of an actual battle of the mobs.

Wherever the gang looked, they saw vacant-eyed zombies creeping toward them. Hannah splashed a potion of strength on the zombies, and they lost many hearts. Noah lunged at the weakened zombies with his diamond sword, destroying them.

"It's going to be a lot harder when you're destroying zombies in front of an audience," Ben remarked as he struck a zombie and destroyed it.

"If I didn't splash those zombies, you'd still be battling them," Hannah reminded him.

More zombies approached the group.

"Oh no! I'll never have time to build the Olympic village." Violet was worried that they'd never get the village ready for the athletes, and she wondered if Daniel was behind this zombie attack. She knew she had to stay focused to get the Olympic Village completed before the opening ceremonies.

Violet hit two zombies, destroying them. She looked at the piles of supplies and hurried over to the wooden planks. Her friends could finish the battle. She had to build. She lifted a plank just as a zombie walked by. Violet reminded herself she ought to battle the hostile mob first for the safety of everyone. She put the wooden plank down. But the zombie was destroyed by Noah's arrow.

"Thanks!" she called out to Noah.

"You have to build, Violet," Noah replied.

The sun began to rise. The zombies disappeared and the friends began to build Olympic Village together. Noah slipped out to enter the tryouts for the Battle of the Mobs. They all wished him good luck.

As Violet constructed the first stadium, a man wearing a green hat and sunglasses appeared in the distance.

"Who is that?" asked Hannah.

He approached the group, and Ben questioned him, "Hi, who are you?"

"I can't believe you don't know who I am," the man with the green hat and sunglasses replied smugly.

4
STADIUMS

"I'm sorry. We don't recognize you," Hannah said politely.

He looked at Violet. "Are you Violet? Nina and Mac sent me here. They said you are constructing a mansion for me."

"A mansion. Nobody told me I was constructing a mansion. I have to build four stadiums, a hotel, and housing for the athletes." Violet pointed at the plans Nina and Mac had given her.

"I can't stay with the others. I need my own place. A mansion," the man with the green hat and sunglasses insisted.

Angela stared at the man and then asked, "Are you Samson?"

"Finally, somebody recognizes me." He smiled.

"Samson is one of the most famous fighters in the Overworld," noted Angela.

"Not *one of* the most famous. I am *the most* famous," he corrected her.

"I don't have any orders to build you a separate house." Violet pointed at the plans again.

"Well, I order you to build a separate house for me. I am the best fighter in the Overworld and I deserve it."

Kaboom! There was an explosion in the distance.

Samson trembled and said quite nervously, "What was that?"

"If you're such a skilled fighter, an explosion shouldn't bother you," said Violet. "Will you stay in the house I am building for all the Olympic athletes if I don't tell anyone you're scared of loud noises?"

"I wasn't scared. And I'm not bothered by TNT. I was just asking why there was an explosion."

"Okay. Fine. You aren't scared. But you must stay with the other athletes. I don't have enough time to build you a separate home," explained Violet.

Ben and Hannah looked out into the distance. They tried to spot the smoke from the explosion, but they couldn't see any.

Violet got back to work. She glanced at Samson, "Are you busy?"

"Well, I have two days until the Olympics. I was going to hone my skills. Why do you ask?"

She handed Samson some granite. "Help me build. It will make you stronger."

Samson looked at the granite. He couldn't believe Violet was asking him to construct a stadium. He was an Olympic star.

"You can't be serious," he said. Samson was shocked at her request.

"Do you want the games to go on?" asked Violet. "Because we have so much work and I have very little help. If you don't put your ego aside, there won't be any games."

Hannah interrupted with, "The Olympic committee is busy trying to secure the town. We might have a potential griefer who wants to destroy the Olympics."

"You aren't talking about Daniel? The griefer who had the rainbow army?" he asked.

"Yes, how do you know him?" questioned Ben.

"He once took over my village. He is the reason I became a skilled fighter. I never want to be attacked by him again. When he found out how strong I had become, he tried to recruit me for his army."

"If you really dislike Daniel, then you should help build this stadium," Violet urged Samson.

Samson didn't reply, but he quietly gathered the supplies Violet handed him and started to build the foundation for the other side of the stadium. The group worked hard and within a few hours, the first stadium was constructed. They stood back and marveled at the grand stadium.

"This is the stadium for the player versus player event," Violet said as she pointed out the room for respawning that was housed right outside the arena.

"This is where I will win my gold medal," Samson said confidently.

"You don't want to jinx yourself by boasting," advised Angela.

"I don't believe in that nonsense. I am the best fighter and I know I'll win." Samson was sure he would walk away with the first-place gold medal.

The sun began to set. Violet wanted to work throughout the night. She had three more stadiums to construct and also the hotel and houses for the athletes. As two Endermen walked past, carrying blocks, Violet and the gang tried to avoid them and to not make eye contact, but it was too late. One of the Endermen shrieked and teleported next to Samson. The gang got a private showing of Samson's skilled fighting. With one strike, the Enderman was destroyed. They were impressed, until a creeper crept up behind Samson. He didn't have time to fight back. The creeper exploded and Samson was destroyed.

"Poor Samson," said Violet, "I wonder where he'll respawn."

"We have to make our way to the tree house," Ben warned them, "before we all get destroyed."

The gang could hear the rattling of skeleton bones. Noah dashed toward the group.

"Stop. Don't shoot!" he called out, worried they might mistake him for a skeleton.

"Noah, help us! We are trying to make our way back to the tree house," shouted Violet.

Noah shot arrows at the skeletons. Hannah splashed the bony beasts with potions. Angela and Ben struck them with their swords. Violet lunged at a skeleton, and with a powerful blow from her enchanted diamond sword she obliterated the hostile mob. Finally the last skeleton was destroyed, and the group raced as fast as they could toward the tree house. When they reached the tree, they stopped in their tracks.

The ladder was missing. The tree house was destroyed. Somebody had blown it up. Rubble lay on the ground around the tree that once held Violet and Noah's scenic tree house.

"We need a place to sleep," Violet said calmly, even though she was devastated.

"Come with me," a voice called out, "I know a place we can stay."

It was Samson. The group didn't know where he had respawned. They also didn't know if they should trust him. But they felt they had no other choice—they followed the skilled fighter through the village and back to the field where the Olympic village was being constructed. He walked the group into the small dwelling Violet had built for the player versus player athletes to respawn in. Samson had crafted a bunch of beds in the room.

"We can all sleep here," suggested Samson.

The gang was extremely tired and everybody climbed into bed. As Violet drifted off to sleep, she wanted to ask Samson how he knew her tree house was destroyed. She looked over at Samson's bed, but he was already asleep. Violet was suspicious, but she was also tired. She couldn't fight the exhaustion and fell asleep. She was happily surprised when she woke up.

5
LET THE GAMES BEGIN

When Violet woke up, her friends were already hard at work on the second stadium.

"Wow!" exclaimed Violet. "Thank you, guys!"

Samson walked over and handed Violet a piece of cake. "I'm so glad you don't mind that we started to work on Olympic Village without you. I was worried that you'd be upset."

"Not at all," Violet replied as she took a bite of cake. "We don't have much time. I appreciate all the help I can get."

Noah joined them. "I am so upset that our house was destroyed. It has to be the work of Daniel. I'm also concerned that he is going to try to destroy the games."

"He probably will try to destroy the games, but we'll stop him." Violet wasn't going to let Daniel ruin the Minecraft Olympics.

"After I respawned in my house outside of town last night, I ran back here and everybody was gone. As I walked through the village looking for you, I saw a man walking alone. I thought it was Daniel. When I approached him, he shielded his face and said, 'Your friends are right up ahead.' Then he ran away. And I could swear I heard him laugh," Samson told them.

Samson's story put Violet's mind at ease. She wanted to trust this world-renowned athlete. She, too, wondered if that was actually Daniel walking around the village last night and what he might be plotting.

"We have to keep an eye out for Daniel," Noah cautioned as he grabbed some more bricks and worked on the stadium for the sprinting competition.

Nina and Mac arrived at the construction site. "Very nice," Nina commented in approval of the two stadiums. "We have some people coming to help you finish Olympic Village. Tomorrow we will have the opening ceremonies and people will be arriving from all around the Overworld."

Violet looked at the patch of land designated to house the hotel and athletes' houses. "I hope we finish in time." She was very worried because there were so many interruptions. And she feared that Daniel would return and cause even greater havoc than a few explosions and some hostile mob attacks.

A group of people in red jackets marched toward the construction site.

"Oh great, they're here!" exclaimed Nina. "These are the workers who will help you finish the village."

Violet couldn't believe her eyes. There were so many people. She had never been in charge of anybody before.

Usually she just asked some friends to help, but now she had to lead an entire construction crew. She felt all jittery.

"You're going to do a terrific job," Mac reassured Violet. "We've seen your other projects, and you're one of the most talented builders in the Overworld. These people are just here to help you finish the job. There's no reason to be nervous."

Violet stood on a block and instructed the crew about what they needed to do to get Olympic Village ready for the games. Everyone got right to work.

Nina and Mac went over the agenda for the opening ceremonies. There would be a parade, fireworks, and a presentation of the top athletes.

"We need to make a big deal when Samson shows up. He's our star athlete," stated Nina.

Noah overheard Nina and interrupted, "Samson's already here." He pointed out Samson carrying granite over to the final stadium that was being constructed.

"What?" Nina questioned. She was shocked.

"How can you have our star athlete building a stadium?" Mac pointed out the absurdity of the situation.

"Samson," Noah called out to his new friend.

Samson put down the granite and walked over to Noah and the others.

"Samson, you don't have to build the stadiums. You can rest for the opening ceremonies and the big fight that you are scheduled to partake in," Mac informed the skilled fighter.

"I don't want to be treated any differently because I'm a skilled fighter. Also, building helps me increase my strength. It's better than sitting around all day and being waited on hand and foot." Samson excused himself and went back to the construction site. He asked Violet what she needed him to do next.

Nina's mouth dropped open. "Wow, that's not the Samson we remember from the last Olympic games."

"I hope this doesn't affect his fight tomorrow. I hope he wins," Noah told them.

"So do we," agreed Nina.

Nina and Mac examined the construction site; they couldn't believe how quickly it was being built. They called Violet over to commend her on the great work.

Violet felt pleased as she looked over the site. A large hotel loomed over the four stadiums. The construction crew was busy building the houses for the athletes. Soon the games would begin.

Athletes and fans started to arrive while the crew placed the finishing touches on Olympic Village. The townspeople and villagers also entered Olympic Village, excited for the games to start. There was a jovial atmosphere everywhere.

Valentino the Butcher showed up with some meat. "Somebody told me they wanted a restaurant."

"Yes," Violet said, and she walked Valentino over to a concession stand she had crafted outside the stadium.

"This is so exciting!" exclaimed Valentino. "I've never been to the Olympic games."

Nina and Mac led the visitors to the hotel. A parade of athletes entered the village. Everybody stopped and cheered as the athletes walked toward their newly erected houses. Samson joined the parade. He had a player versus player battle to fight. Violet and her friends hoped he'd win.

Violet lit torches and placed them on the walls of the stadiums to prevent hostile mobs from spawning in Olympic Village. The construction crew had also built a large iron golem to watch over the village.

As the evening set in, everyone felt safe in the well-lit Olympic Village. Nina and Mac stood in the center of the village and announced the official start of the Olympic games.

The sky lit up with a fantastic display of fireworks. Red and green fireworks shot up like giant fountains of light. Violet had never seen anything so beautiful. She had also never felt this comfortable outdoors in the nighttime. It seemed like the entire Overworld was watching the fireworks show. Everybody cheered. Despite the cheering and the noise from the fireworks, Violet was sure she heard a boom in the distance.

Noah rushed over to Violet's side. "Did you hear that noise?"

Kaboom! Another explosion split the air.

"Yes," Violet said fearfully, "and it doesn't sound like fireworks. I wonder what Daniel has destroyed."

"We don't know it's definitely Daniel," replied Noah.

"There's only one way to find out." Violet dashed out of Olympic Village and toward their town. Noah followed, and they made their way through the darkness, hoping they wouldn't be attacked by hostile mobs lurking in the shadows.

6
FIREWORKS AND
FIERY BEASTS

Noah and Violet raced through the village, but they couldn't find the place where the TNT had ignited.

"We should head back to the Olympic games. This is a fool's errand." Noah could hear the celebratory noises from the Olympic games and he wanted to return. Also, he had never slept in a hotel before, and he was excited to spend the night in the Olympic hotel they had constructed.

"I guess you're right." Violet felt almost ready to give up. They had searched the entire village and everything seemed to be intact. As they made their way through the town, Violet noticed some rubble.

"The library!" Noah called out.

The library had been blown up. Somebody had also blown up Valentino's butcher shop.

"Valentino's shop!" cried Violet.

"He'll be so upset," lamented Noah.

"We should go back to the games. We have to tell Nina and Mac," Violet said. She wanted the Olympic committee to watch over the town. Now that everyone was distracted with the games, it was the perfect time for Daniel to destroy their town.

"Yes, I have to tell Valentino about his butcher shop." Noah followed Violet as they trekked through the dark streets toward the festive village that stood just feet from their town.

Violet weaved among the crowd until she reached Nina and Mac, and she gave them the bad news about the explosions.

"We must increase security for the games," declared Nina.

"But we also shouldn't stop celebrating," said Mac.

As those words fell from Mac's mouth, a roar was heard louder than the crackle of the fireworks.

Everyone looked up, as the Ender Dragon swept into the crowd. Cheers turned to cries. Noah and Violet each grabbed their bows and arrows and shot at the dragon.

The dragon's black wings struck a group of bystanders. Ben dashed through the crowd and threw a snowball at the evil beast. The Ender Dragon flew directly at Ben, striking him. Ben was destroyed.

"Ben!" Hannah cried as she grabbed a snowball from her inventory and aimed at the dragon.

Noah and Violet shot arrows. The Olympic spectators started to take weapons from the inventories and joined in the battle. Arrows flew through the air, and some spectators advanced toward the dragon, trying to strike the flying menace with their swords. The Ender Dragon began to lose its energy. There were no Ender crystals to help the dragon regain its strength. It grew weaker with each strike. Hannah continued to throw snowballs at the dragon. She looked at the dragon's vicious purple eyes, and threw her final snowball. The beast roared.

Suddenly the dragon exploded, lighting up the night sky like fireworks. The crowd cheered. The real fireworks show continued. After the spectacular finale, Nina stood on a podium and addressed the crowd.

"I'd like to welcome you all to the Minecraft Olympics." Nina scanned the crowd. "I also want to apologize for the Ender Dragon. I know it wasn't my fault, but I still feel bad about it. There are some people who'd like to see the games cancelled and to scare everyone. We aren't going to let this happen. We are going to continue with the games."

Everyone cheered!

Mac walked up onto the podium and stood next to Nina. "Tomorrow the first event begins. It's a player versus player competition. This event promises to be one of the most exciting Olympic battles."

The crowd cheered again! As the spectators cleared out and some headed back to the hotel while the townspeople walked to their homes, everyone gazed up into the night sky. They watched for the Ender Dragon or the Wither. After the dragon attack, they had to be prepared for what might come next. Although everybody was excited for the player versus player games, they all felt as if they were engaging in their own personal battle against this evil force that wanted to destroy the Minecraft Olympics.

Violet and Noah strolled toward the hotel. Violet said to her friend, "I really hope the games will go on tomorrow and Daniel won't disrupt Samson's battle."

Noah agreed. They both stopped when they reached the front door of the hotel. Noah looked around the entrance. "It would take a lot of TNT to blow this place up. I don't think Daniel can destroy it."

Violet hoped Noah was right, as she entered the hotel and headed to her room, hoping to get some sleep before the first games began.

7
PLAYER VS. PLAYER

Warm sunshine streamed through the window of the hotel. Violet hopped out of bed to catch an early morning view of Olympic Village. Crowds were already standing outside the stadium. She saw Samson being ushered through the crowd. Violet wondered who he'd battle that morning.

"Violet," Noah called from the other side of the hotel door. Violet opened the door and Noah handed her a piece of cake.

"Thanks," she said and took a big bite. "Let's go see Samson's battle."

Noah and Violet walked to the stadium. Violet could see Nina standing by the entrance greeting the crowds.

"Violet and Noah," Nina called to them, "we reserved special seats for you." Nina showed them to their seats. They were in front, right by the arena. To the left was the room where the player who was defeated would respawn.

Violet hoped Samson wouldn't be the one who had to respawn.

A man stepped up onto the arena, wearing a red Olympic jacket with an official badge sewn on the pocket. He took out a megaphone and announced, "The first battle is between all-star Samson and his opponent Finn."

The man walked away and the two fighters entered the arena. Samson and Finn carried diamond swords and wore shiny diamond armor. Finn struck Samson with his enchanted sword, but Samson was able to shield himself from the blow and hit Finn. Finn lost a heart. As Samson threw a splash potion of weakness on Finn, he also struck his opponent with his sword. Finn was losing energy quickly. He tried to fight back, but Samson was able to avoid all of Finn's hits. Samson delivered a final blow. Finn was destroyed. The audience cheered. Samson was the winner! People began to call out Samson's name in unison: "Sam-son, Sam-son!"

Finn respawned in the special room and reentered the arena. Samson thanked Finn for a great battle, and then Finn exited the arena.

The man in the red jacket returned to the arena and announced Samson's second opponent: "Samson will now battle Dash!"

Dash also entered the arena wearing diamond armor and carrying a diamond sword.

The battle between Dash and Samson was intense. Samson was still recovering from his first battle with Finn, and accidentally let Dash strike him with a diamond sword. This was unusual for Samson—he usually avoided getting hit by anybody during a battle. Samson began to fight back. He struck Dash several times until he weakened him and then destroyed him.

"Another victory for Samson!" the man in the red jacket called out to the crowd. The audience was going wild. They were standing up and cheering Samson on. "There's only one more fighter. If Samson beats him, he wins the gold medal." Then the man in the red jacket announced, "Let's all welcome Peter, one of the Overworld's most daring fighters!"

Violet's heart beat fast. She wondered what made this fighter so daring. She wanted Samson to win the gold medal and to be declared the winner of the player versus player games. But her heart sunk when she saw a very large man enter the arena. He wasn't wearing diamond armor. Before the battle began he asked Samson if he would fight without armor.

Samson paused. The audience looked at him. "Uh-uh-uh," Samson began to stutter, "I guess so. But I've never fought without armor."

Samson reluctantly took off his armor. He didn't want to battle this way, but if he refused, the audience would be disappointed and the battle would be unfair. *You can't fight an unarmored opponent when you are wearing armor*, Samson thought. He placed his diamond armor on the ground. The fight began!

Samson struck Peter with the sword. Getting the first hit gave Samson a lot of confidence. Peter was caught off guard when Samson struck him, so Samson used the opportunity to pound Peter again. As Peter regained his strength, Samson splashed a potion of weakness on the large man. Then Samson struck Peter two more times, and Peter was destroyed.

Peter respawned in the special room, and he made his way back to the arena. He watched as the man in the red jacket gave Samson a skin with a gold medal and declared him the winner.

"Samson. You are the master fighter of the Overworld. You are now an Olympic gold medalist! Wear this medal with pride!"

The crowd cheered. But their joyous calls didn't drown out the sound that boomed in the distance.

Kaboom!

There was a loud explosion. The crowds made their way out of the stadium and were devastated to see the stadium that was built for the Battle of the Mobs had been blown up.

"I guess Daniel has more TNT than we realized," Violet groaned as she looked at the rubble.

"I was so excited that I was chosen to compete in the Battle of the Mobs," Noah said despondently, "but I guess I can't just think about myself. This affects a lot more people than me. We have to do something and stop Daniel."

Violet agreed. She looked at the crowd. She wondered if Daniel was working alone or if his rainbow griefer army was lurking around the town. This was a hard job to pull off on his own.

Valentino the Butcher hurried over to Noah and Violet. "First my shop and now the stadium," he cried.

"We will rebuild the stadium," Noah declared quite loudly and the crowd overheard and cheered him on.

"Yes, we will," added Valentino, "but I have something very important to tell you. I saw something while I was working at the concession stand outside the stadium."

"What did you see?" Violet asked. She wondered if Valentino could offer them a clue and help them to find Daniel and whoever else was behind these vicious attacks.

"When I was at the concession stand, I saw two men wearing official red Olympic jackets standing right by the stadium, seconds before it exploded. I'm sure that one of them was carrying a brick of TNT." Valentino told this all in one breath.

"I bet the griefers are disguised as Olympic officials," Violet theorized, "so we don't recognize them."

"I'd recognize Daniel anywhere," Samson volunteered as he joined the group, wearing his shiny new gold medal skin.

"I'm sure you would," Violet replied. "But what if it isn't Daniel? What if he has someone working for him?"

The group looked out at the various Olympic workers wearing red jackets. Any one of these people could be working for Daniel. They didn't know which one to question first. And they certainly didn't know whom they could trust. Nina and Mac walked over to the Noah and Violet.

"What happened?" asked Mac.

As Violet told them what Valentino had seen, she wondered if she could trust Nina and Mac. *Maybe they are working with Daniel?* she thought. Questions spun around in Violet's head as she watched the crowds make their way in the direction of the sprinting competition that was about to start.

8

SPRINTING TO THE FINISH

"We need to make sure the stadium where the sprinting competition is taking place is secure," Nina stated as the crowds flocked toward the entrance. "I don't want that stadium exploding with people in it!"

"Yes," Mac agreed and headed for the stadium with the security personnel.

Noah and Violet followed behind with Nina. She showed them to their seats.

"It looks like we have VIP seats at every game," Violet said, as Nina led them to front row seats.

"Yes, you built these stadiums," said Nina. "You deserve the best view."

"What about the Battle of the Mobs stadium? Shouldn't we leave now? I have to start reconstructing that stadium." Violet worried that she shouldn't be watching the games but helping to rebuild the Olympic village.

"We will do that after the sprinting competition. I don't want any of the games to be disturbed because of Daniel. He doesn't deserve that much attention. These games must go on," Nina told Violet.

An Olympic official stood on the track and shot an arrow into the air. The games had begun. Six runners began their sprint around the track. Violet and the audience cheered for the runners. Two of the runners were neck in neck. Violet wondered if it would be a tie as the runners approached the finish line.

Kaboom!

"What was that?" Violet shouted.

Noah dashed for the exit and Violet followed. When Violet reached the exit and stood by Valentino's concession stand, her mouth gaped in horror.

"Oh no!" Violet cried, "Watch out, Valentino!"

The courtyard outside the stadium was filled with creepers. They exploded, destroying many of the people running for shelter around Olympic Village. Noah pulled out his bow and arrow and shot at the green explosive mobs that filled Olympic Village. Violet called to Ben, Hannah, Angela, and Jack. Together they battled the creepers, narrowly avoiding getting caught in the flames.

When the final creeper was destroyed, Violet sighed. As she looked out at the empty courtyard, she saw someone with a red jacket hurry past the stadium she had built for the archery competition.

"Come with me," she called out to her friends.

When Violet reached the archery stadium, the red-jacketed Olympic official was missing.

"What are we looking for?" asked Ben.

"I think Daniel is dressed like an Olympic official and is causing all of this trouble. I thought I spotted him running over here." Violet entered the stadium.

"I see someone!" Hannah shouted when she saw a man with a red jacket sneak backstage.

Carrying diamond swords, the gang made their way onto the stage and then through the back door.

"Stop!" Noah screamed at the man.

The man in the red Olympic jacket was banging into the ground with his pickaxe.

"Be careful, there's lava under this stadium," warned Violet. She had encountered a large lava flow when she was constructing the stadium.

"Why are you warning him?" Ben asked, shocked. He wanted this evil man to fall into the lava.

The man looked up and questioned, "Who are you?"

"We could ask you the same question," Violet said, and she approached him with her diamond sword.

"I am helping to finish this stadium," the man replied.

"You're lying. I was in charge of building this stadium and know everyone who worked on the project." Violet was angry.

"But I was sent here, because . . ." he paused.

"Don't make anything up. You were sent here because you had to summon creepers for Daniel. Well, it's over now." Violet brought her diamond sword closer to the man's chest. "You aren't even wearing diamond armor. With a couple of blows, I can utterly destroy you."

The man stared at her diamond sword and confessed, "You're right. I was sent here to summon more hostile mobs. Daniel was planning to distract you with rain and a zombie invasion while he blew up the remaining stadiums. I don't even want to be a part of this. He is forcing me."

Violet didn't know if she should believe this stranger. "How can he force you to do these evil acts?"

"He captured me when I was treasure hunting. He took everything from me, and told me the only way he'd set me free was if I helped him destroy the Minecraft Olympics."

"Don't you know you are hurting innocent people?" Ben questioned, and he pointed his diamond sword at the man.

"We can help you," Violet told the stranger.

Her friends looked at Violet in surprise.

"Help him?" Hannah felt confused.

"Yes, if he leads us to Daniel and helps us stop the attack, we can set him free and he can continue to lead a life as a treasure hunter," replied Violet.

The man seemed excited. "Yes, please let me help you. My name is Trent."

The gang walked toward the exit of the archery stadium with the red-jacketed man. As soon as they stepped outside, the sky grew dark and rain fell.

"Stop the rain!" Violet demanded.

Trent looked at her and said, "I can't. It's too late. But I can help you stop the explosion. I know where Daniel hides the TNT."

Zombies lumbered toward Olympic Village. The spectators and Olympic officials battled the undead hostile mob that disrupted the Olympic games, as Violet and the gang followed Daniel's minion toward the TNT. Violet walked behind Trent and hoped he wasn't leading them into a trap.

9

PLAY BY THE RULES

Trent led the gang outside of Olympic Village. There was a small wooden structure in the distance. He walked toward the building and opened the door.

"Oh my," Violet said, and she followed him in. "I've never seen this much TNT."

Noah had an idea. "Let's blow up this building. It's far enough from Olympic Village that it won't cause any damage to the stadiums."

"I'll do it," offered Trent.

The gang left the building before Trent ignited the TNT.

Kaboom!

The wooden structure exploded, and the gang started back to the Olympic games. Trent followed them.

As they reached Olympic Village, the sun came out, and the zombies were gone.

"What else was he planning?" asked Violet.

"I don't know. This was the only part that I was involved in," confessed Trent, "but there are others working with Daniel. He is conspiring with someone who is in the Olympics."

"It must be either Nina or Mac. They are the ones who are in charge of these Olympic games," Violet thought out loud.

"No," said Trent. "It's not an official. It's an athlete."

The group stood in silence, pondering his words, as Samson called to them in the distance and ran toward them.

"I've been looking all over for you guys," Samson said to his friends. He was still wearing his gold medal.

Violet wondered if Samson was the one working with Daniel. Then she remembered Samson talking about how he despised Daniel. And he had helped construct the village and seemed so proud of his gold medal. They had to trust Samson.

"Someone is trying to destroy these games," Noah told Samson.

"I've noticed that," Samson agreed. He looked at the rubble from the stadium that had been destroyed.

Nina and Mac hurried over. Mac announced, "We have to begin rebuilding the stadium for the Battle of the Mobs. I don't want any further interruptions. I want the games to go on."

"Who are you?" Nina asked as she looked at Trent. "You're not an Olympic official."

"No, he isn't," explained Violet. "He admitted to working with Daniel."

"How did you get that jacket?" Nina inquired.

"Um, I don't know. Daniel gave it to me," Trent replied nervously.

"Trent also told us some very disturbing news," added Violet.

"What?" asked Nina.

Trent began to talk. "I'm not the only one working with Daniel. I know he has an athlete who is working with him. They plan on destroying the Olympics, but I'm not sure how they plan on doing it."

"Who is it?" Nina was shocked and upset.

"I don't know," admitted Trent.

"We have to find out who is working with Daniel. Every athlete is a suspect now." Nina eyed Samson as she spoke.

"Do you think *I* am working with Daniel?" Samson was mad. "I would never side with him. He's awful."

Violet looked up at the sky; evening was approaching. "We need to start reconstructing the stadium for the battle tomorrow. It's almost nighttime. I don't want to build in the dark."

"That's a good idea. And I will find out what athlete is working with Daniel," Nina stated, and she rushed off toward the Olympic hotel with Mac.

Violet and her friends began to reconstruct the stadium. As they built the first wall, they placed torches on the side of the wall for safety. They spent most of the night building the stadium. When it was completed, the group made their way back to the hotel to get some rest before the next day.

"Tomorrow, you'll be battling hostile mobs in the stadium that we built," Violet told Noah.

"It's hard to be excited for the battle when we are also being attacked by Daniel," Noah replied.

Samson smiled and said, "Noah, you're going to do a great job. I've seen you fight a bunch of hostile mobs."

Violet and Noah stood together in front of the hotel with Samson. Noah thanked him and said, "I'm going to try my best."

Samson stared at the athlete's housing. "I can't believe someone who is participating in the Olympics is also trying to destroy it. It doesn't make any sense."

"When you head back to your room, you should look for potential suspects." Violet eyed the entrance of the athlete's headquarters.

Samson agreed and he left Noah and Violet. As Violet entered the hotel, she thought she heard a noise and quickly turned around, but there was nothing there.

"Did you hear something?" asked Violet.

"Yes, it sounded like something exploded," said Noah.

The duo sprinted back toward the town. They needed to see what had happened. As they reached the village streets, they were shocked to see Daniel standing in front of them, waving his diamond sword. An army of Endermen carrying blocks trailed behind him.

"You destroyed my TNT!" he shouted at them.

"TNT was made to explode," Noah taunted him.

"You stole my army." Daniel quickly pulled out a splash potion and threw it on Noah and Violet. They were left extremely weak. Daniel called to the Endermen. Loud shrieks filled the air as dozens of Endermen teleported toward Noah and Violet. They were trapped.

"Over here!" Hannah called to her friends.

Noah and Violet could see Hannah, Ben, and Angela rush toward the Endermen. They struck the Endermen with their diamond swords. Jack and Samson were carrying large buckets.

"Stand back!" Samson shouted and threw a bucket of lava on the Endermen. But it was too late. Noah and Violet were destroyed.

"What happened?" Violet asked her friend, when she respawned in the hotel.

"Daniel's Endermen destroyed us," explained Noah.

The bright sun shined through the window. "It's morning," Violet remarked. "We have to find Daniel."

"We do. But I also have to participate in the Battle of the Mobs," Noah reminded Violet.

"We can't miss that. We can't let Daniel stop the Olympic games." Violet hurried out of the hotel, ready to see her friend compete in his first Olympic game.

Kaboom!

As Violet and Noah stepped outside the hotel, they saw the athletes' housing explode.

"Samson!" Violet shouted, but there was no response. She hoped he wasn't in the building.

10
BATTLE OF THE MOBS

Violet and Noah rushed toward the athletes' housing, searching for Samson. Mac and Nina raced behind them.

"Don't worry," explained Mac. "There are no athletes in the building. They were eating breakfast in the stadium and preparing for the games."

"But who blew it up?" asked Violet.

"We've kept the man in the red jacket you discovered as our prisoner. We are asking him questions, but he doesn't seem to know who caused this explosion," said Mac.

"We are still looking for the athlete who wants to destroy the games," Nina informed them.

"We saw Daniel last night." As Violet spoke, Nina stood frozen.

"You saw Daniel?" Nina couldn't believe what she heard.

"Yes, he tried to attack us with his army of Endermen. There were so many of them, and they started to shriek and teleport. Hannah, Ben, Angela, Jack, and Samson tried to save us, but they couldn't."

"What happened to your friends?" asked Nina. "Were they able to stop Daniel?"

Violet paused. She wasn't sure. "I don't know where they are."

"We have to find them. They may have the answers we need." Nina was about to leave for the town when Hannah and Ben walked toward them.

"What happened to the athletes' housing?" Ben asked, looking at the rubble.

"Somebody blew it up," Violet replied as she looked at Ben and Hannah. "What happened to you last night? Did Daniel destroy you?"

"No," Ben explained. "After you were destroyed and we were able to get rid of the pesky Endermen, we tried to destroy Daniel. But he splashed a potion of invisibility on himself and sprinted away."

"I wonder where he's hiding," said Nina.

"We will find out, but we need to get back to the games. We have the third game scheduled for today," Mac reminded them.

"I know!" Noah was excited, "I'm in the game."

"But we aren't going to start with the Battle of the Mobs. We have to repeat the sprinting competition. We were never able to declare a winner," Nina told them as they walked toward the stadium where the sprinting competition was about to begin.

Violet and Noah took their seats and watched the runners line up for the second day in a row. Violet eyed the runners at the starting line, wondering if any of those athletes were working with Daniel. The start-of-the-race arrow flew into the air and the sprinters began to race around the track. Again, there were two runners who were running at the same pace. They continued to run very close together as they approached the finish line. Finally one of the runners quickly picked up speed and won the race. Cheers erupted throughout the arena.

"We have a winner!" The Olympic official announced his name and placed a gold medal skin on the sprinter.

The crowds left the stadium to watch the Battle of the Mobs next. Noah walked over to the stadium with Violet. She could tell he was nervous.

"Are you ready for the battle?" Violet smiled at her friend.

"Yes, but I wish they told me what hostile mob I have to battle," confessed Noah.

"I will be cheering from the audience," said Violet.

She had to admit, she was also nervous for Noah. They parted ways and he headed into the stadium's entrance for athletes.

Hannah, Ben, Angela, and Jack sat in the front row with Violet. They cheered when Noah's name was finally called after all other competitors had gone and he stepped onto the stage.

Noah wore diamond armor and carried a diamond sword.

An Olympic official announced: "Let the battle begin!"

Within seconds, Noah was surrounded by a group of skeletons shooting arrows at him. Noah dodged the arrows as he struck the skeletons with his sword, and splashed them with a potion. When the final skeleton was destroyed, the Olympic official announced: "Noah only lost one heart!"

The audience cheered!

Before Noah could relax, the official called out, "Round 2!"

A cluster of zombies lumbered toward Noah. Again, Noah avoided being hit and struck the zombies with his sword, destroying them.

The audience went wild!

The final and third round was tricky. Both slimes and spiders filled the stage. Noah struck a slime with his sword, creating smaller slime cubes, which he tried to battle while he struck the numerous spiders that crawled on the floor of the stage. Noah was losing energy and feared he'd lose the final round. He struck the smaller cubes, destroying them, and obliterated the spiders. Just when he thought the round was over, a witch spawned on the stage and charged at him, splashing him with a potion. Noah felt very weak.

The crowd cheered for Noah, shouting at him that he could win the battle.

Noah didn't believe the crowd. He was weak and wasn't sure he had the strength to battle the evil witch. As he stood in front of the witch, he could hear Violet and his friends cheer. Noah used what little strength he had and struck the witch with his diamond sword until she was destroyed. He was shocked when the Olympic official patted his shoulder and said, "Noah is our gold medal winner!"

Noah loved feeling the weight from the gold medal. He looked at the shiny medal and smiled.

"You did it, Noah!" Violet ran to the stage with the others. They were so proud.

"We have matching medals," Samson said with a smile. "Good job, Noah!"

"Now, we have to go find Daniel," Noah told his friends.

"I think you need to replenish your energy first." Violet gave Noah some carrots and milk.

"Thanks!" He took a sip of the milk and a bite of the carrot.

Violet noticed Mac talking to an athlete in the corner. It was one of the sprinters she had seen at the morning's competition. The sprinter exited the stadium, and Violet quietly followed him.

She saw the sprinter head in the direction of the archery stadium, where the final competition would be held the following morning. He entered the stadium. She walked closely behind, but she was very quiet and careful so he didn't notice her.

Violet followed him into the back of the arena, where he met two men in red Olympic jackets. She hid behind a wall as she watched the men. She was shocked when she recognized one of the men. It was Daniel.

"We see you, Violet," Daniel called out with a sinister laugh. "There's no need to hide."

Violet tried to sprint away, but Daniel caught up to her. She was trapped.

11
REVENGE ISN'T SWEET

Violet wished she could call for help, but it was useless. She was alone. Violet grabbed her diamond sword and struck Daniel, but he shielded himself and then struck her with his sword.

"There's no need to fight me." Daniel let out another laugh.

"My friends are going to find me here. You'll never get away with this," Violet said fervently.

"Get away with what? What do you think I'm doing, Violet?"

"You're evil."

"You were the one who stole my army. You and your pesky friend Noah have destroyed everything I ever built. You ruined my life." Daniel was infuriated.

"Ruined your life? You were building a life by hurting other people. You're not a nice person," Violet shouted, and she bolted away from Daniel.

He ran after her. When she reached the exit, she saw Noah and Hannah.

"Help!" Violet called out.

Her friends spotted her, and they saw Daniel standing behind her with his diamond sword.

"Watch out!" shouted Noah.

Daniel struck Violet with his sword. She began losing energy. Noah rushed toward them. He stopped to shoot an arrow at Daniel, which landed on Daniel's arm.

Nina and Mac noticed Daniel and they also raced toward him. Nina had her sword out.

"You're destroying the Olympic games," Nina said as she lunged for Daniel and struck him with her sword.

Daniel called out, "Mac, stop her!"

Mac struck Nina with his sword.

Nina was shocked and she gasped, "What are you doing?"

"I work for Daniel now!" Mac struck Nina again.

Ben and Samson hit Mac with their swords. "You're a traitor," they shouted at him.

"No! He understands why I want revenge," Daniel defended Mac. "He used to be a rainbow griefer."

Jack rushed at Daniel. "So was I. And I know how badly you treat people. You don't deserve to act out any plans of revenge on anyone. You deserve to be punished."

Daniel struck Jack and splashed a potion of harming on him. Jack was destroyed.

"What did you do to Jack?" Violet was angry.

As the gang continued to battle Mac and Daniel, Violet noticed the sprinter from the competition exit the stadium. She wondered where he was going and decided to follow him. Noah trailed behind Violet, his gold medal clanging against his diamond armor as he raced out of the stadium.

A purple light flashed across the sky. It was the Wither.

"The Olympics are over now," Daniel called out from the stadium. "I've summoned the Wither."

The three-headed beast flew through the sky and shot skulls at the crowd. Noah and Violet shot as many arrows as they could at this evil beast.

"The Wither is so hard to destroy," Violet cried as a wither skull hit her body and she was struck with the Wither effect.

Hannah and Ben joined them to help battle the Wither. "Daniel got away," Ben informed them.

"How?" Noah was upset.

"He has some secret tunnel built underneath the stadium. We saw the hole. Nina and Samson are trying to find him." Hannah's news burst out in one breath while she shot arrows at the Wither.

"How is it possible? I thought there was lava underneath the stadium?" said Violet. One of her arrows struck and weakened the Wither. She was happy with the progress, but she wanted the Wither to finally get destroyed.

"The Wither is hard to battle. You need patience and strength," Noah reminded her as he aimed at the Wither and struck it.

"It's hard to be patient when I know Daniel is still in an underground tunnel," she explained. Violet wanted this to be over. She wanted Daniel to get caught and the Olympics to go on as scheduled. She was tired of fighting. She missed the festive fireworks display and the excitement of building Olympic Village. Daniel was ruining one of the best events to happen in the town. The Olympics were epic and he was destroying them.

Snowballs, arrows, and the occasional blow from a diamond sword eventually weakened the Wither. Hannah shot an arrow at the beast, but it struck her with a wither skull. Noah gave her some milk to ward off the Wither effect.

Violet's arrow hit the Wither and it was destroyed, dropping a Nether star. Hannah picked it up. "We can use this to craft beacons," she told the others and placed it in her inventory.

Violet grabbed some potion of healing and took a sip, handing the bottle to the others. "We need to be strong. We have to find Daniel and stop him."

"I can't believe we trusted Mac and he was working with Daniel the whole time," Hannah remarked as they headed for the stadium.

"I know," Violet agreed. "We have to stop him, too."

The gang entered the stadium, but it was filling up with spectators.

"I thought the archery competition wasn't until tomorrow." Violet looked around the stadium. "This doesn't make sense. Why are people here?"

Then Violet saw an Olympic official standing on stage announcing the archery competition would be performed that afternoon.

Violet didn't trust him. She knew this was one of Daniel's tricks. She had to warn everyone. She jumped up onto the stage.

"The competition schedule hasn't been changed," Violet told the man who made the announcement.

"Stop. You don't know what you're talking about," he said to Violet.

"Nina is the one in charge of the Olympics and she never told me about a change," Violet shouted.

"Mac told me to announce the change to the schedule," the man defended himself.

Violet was very nervous. She knew Mac was working with Daniel. She grabbed the megaphone from the man's hand and shouted, "Everyone exit the stadium."

Someone in the crowd screamed, "Endermites!"

Another person shouted, "Silverfish!"

The stadium was infested with hostile insects. The crowd rushed out of the stadium as they sheltered themselves from the insects that were biting the spectators.

Violet and her friends were the only ones who stayed behind. They searched for the hole in the ground that would lead them to Daniel.

"I think I found it!" Hannah called out.

There was a small hole behind the stage. Hannah crawled into the passage. Violet and the others followed. They didn't know what to expect, but they knew they had to find Daniel, and they had to do it fast.

Violet was surprised to hear a familiar voice call out to her, "Violet, come over here."

12
DOWN THE HOLE

"**W**here?" Violet asked, with her friends at her side.

"Just farther down the tunnel. Light a torch," Nina called out to Violet.

Violet lit a torch and spotted a cave spider. She struck it with her sword.

"And watch out for cave spiders," warned Nina.

"I see them!" Violet looked down and saw more cave spiders crawling on the floor.

"I think there is a cave spider spawner down here," Nina said as she walked over to Violet.

"I bet Daniel has this place booby trapped," Noah said as he stared down the long dark hallway.

"Do you know where Daniel is hiding?" asked Hannah.

"I lost him." Nina was disappointed. "I was just trying to find you guys when you came down the hole."

"We're going to find him together," Noah reassured Nina.

Violet was afraid to ask. "What happened to Samson?"

"Daniel destroyed him; I barely escaped. I believe there's a stronghold attached to this tunnel and that is where Daniel, Mac, and the sprinter are hiding."

Noah walked beside Nina, leading them down the tunnel toward the door that might lead to the stronghold. When they reached the door Nina pulled it open.

"It is a stronghold!" she exclaimed, and the gang followed her inside.

"This is very similar to the stronghold Daniel had in the frozen biome," Violet noted as she made her way into the large room with a staircase.

"We have to be very quiet," Noah said, "and we can't look for treasure."

"I'm sure everything has been looted," said Hannah.

"Watch out!" shouted Nina in terror.

The gang raced out of the stronghold and into the hall as fast as they could. Someone had flooded the stronghold with lava. The lava wave inched closer to the gang as they quickly made their way to the exit.

Noah was the last to climb out of the hole. "We made it," he said in relief.

"Yes, but we're back where we started." Violet was upset. She wanted to capture Daniel so the Olympics could go on without any incidents.

"Guys!" Samson called to his friends, "You need to come with me!"

The gang sprinted over to Samson who stood by the entrance to the stadium. "Look!" he cried.

The Olympic square was filled with Endermen, and they began to attack the spectators and athletes. The

Endermen's high-pitched shrieks were piercing and painful to hear. Violet wanted to cover her ears, but she had to be prepared to battle.

An Enderman shrieked and teleported to her side. She grabbed her diamond sword and struck it. Noah also struck the weakened Enderman, destroying it.

"I have a plan," Noah told Violet. "Get your pickaxe."

Noah and Violet banged their pickaxes into the ground, reaching a lava flow that lay right beneath the ground's surface.

"We need some buckets!" Noah called out to Hannah.

The trio carefully gathered lava into the buckets, while their friends and the spectators battled the Endermen invasion with swords, arrows, and potions. Noah, Violet, and Hannah warned their friends and spectators to stand back. They dumped buckets of lava on the Endermen, destroying the entire crop of lanky beasts that attacked the Olympic spectators.

Hannah accidentally got lava on herself.

"Hannah!" Violet cried.

It was too late—the lava destroyed Hannah. Violet was devastated, but she looked at the hotel. "Thankfully, the hotel hasn't been destroyed, so Hannah will respawn."

"It's just a matter of time before all of the buildings are destroyed," Nina lamented. She stared at the rubble from the athletes' housing. "I can't believe I was working with Mac and he was actually one of Daniel's minions. Why did I trust him?"

"It's not your fault. None of us had any idea that Mac was working with Daniel," Violet consoled Nina.

"We will make sure nothing else gets blown up," declared Noah.

Violet hoped that was the case, but she wasn't sure. Now that she knew Daniel had so many people working for him, she was even more worried. She wondered what he was planning next. Violet walked to the prison where Nina and Mac had placed Trent. When she reached the prison cell, it was empty. *Mac must have freed him. Now there were more people working with Daniel,* she thought. Violet began to imagine all of the horrid things Daniel and his new group of griefers could stage at the Olympics. She thought about the archery competition. She wanted the game to go on, but she worried that it was too dangerous.

Evening set in. Violet wasn't even scared of the dark anymore. After battling Endermen in the daylight and having to fight both the Ender Dragon and the Wither, she felt like an expert fighter. Also, her best friend was the gold medal winner of the Battle of the Mobs. She knew that whatever crept her way in the dark of night, she would be able to conquer it. She hoped she could also conquer Daniel.

"Violet," Noah's voice boomed through Olympic Village. "We need your help!"

Violet rushed over to her friend. She wondered what was coming next.

13
GAME ON!

"**N**ina wants the games to go on tomorrow. The archery competition is the final event at the Olympics. She also wants to make sure the stadium is secure," Noah told Violet as they walked to the stadium.

Violet saw someone rush past—a spider jockey was chasing them. Noah shot an arrow at the skeleton riding the spider.

"Trent!" Violet shouted at the man who was rushing from the spider jockey.

"I escaped!" he called out to Violet. "Mac was keeping me prisoner because I wanted to help destroy Daniel."

Violet shot an arrow at the spider jockey, but she wondered if she should trust Trent. She knew they had to destroy the spider jockey before questioning Trent. If not, it would be the end of them.

Noah also shot an arrow at the skeleton, but it was bony and the strikes didn't affect the skeleton.

Violet bravely lunged forward, striking the red-eyed evil spider with her sword. Trent followed closely behind Violet, and he too delivered a blow to the spider. The spider was destroyed. It dropped a spider eye. Violet placed this valuable find in her inventory.

Noah singlehandedly battled the skeleton. He struck it with his diamond sword. The skeleton fought back, but it was no match for one of Noah's strong potions, which he splashed on the bony terror. The skeleton was destroyed and dropped an arrow, which Noah placed in his inventory.

"I see Daniel!" Trent called to Noah and Violet.

Daniel sprinted through the Olympic square carrying blocks of TNT. Violet, Noah, and Trent raced after him, shooting arrows.

Daniel placed the blocks of TNT on the ground. As the group approached him, he ignited the bricks.

Kaboom! A fiery explosion rocked the Olympic square, but Daniel didn't destroy Noah, Violet, and Trent as he had hoped.

"He went that way!" Noah called to his friends, and he watched Daniel dash out of the Olympic village and toward the grassy biome that was outside the village.

"Daniel has a house right near here," Trent told them. "He built it near the building where he stored the TNT."

"You mean the building we exploded?" asked Violet.

"Yes," replied Trent. "I bet he's very upset about that. We destroyed a lot of TNT."

"It looks like he still has more blocks. I wonder where he's getting all of these explosives?" Noah questioned as they hurried behind Daniel. They tried to catch up but he was quite fast.

"You'll never win!" Daniel looked back at them and let out a sinister laugh.

"Don't let him scare you. We will win. He's an evil bully and we'll stop him, and the Olympics will continue," Trent said. He was furious with Daniel.

Daniel ran farther away from Olympic Village, heading for the swampy biome.

"I hate going to the swamp at night," confessed Violet. "It really creeps me out."

"We just have to stick together," Noah reassured her.

"Look at Daniel," Trent said, as he watched Daniel battle a witch that had spawned from a hut. She threw a potion at Daniel and rambled toward him.

"We need to stop her. We don't want Daniel to get destroyed. We want to capture him." Violet charged at the witch and struck her with a diamond sword.

Noah and Trent shot arrows at the witch. Daniel, who was weakened by the witch's potion, stood motionless. He was confused. He didn't understand why Violet, Noah, and Trent were helping him. He assumed they'd want him to be destroyed at the hand of the purple-robed swamp witch.

The witch was destroyed and she dropped a potion of healing, which Noah placed in his inventory.

Trent walked over to the weakened Daniel. He placed his diamond sword close to Daniel and said, "You are done terrorizing the Olympics. You are done hurting innocent people."

"Innocent?" Daniel defended himself. "These people aren't innocent. Most of that town is filled with traitors. They were working for me. They were a part of my army, and they abandoned me to live with Violet and Noah."

"You are mean to people and force them to do bad things. How can you say bad things about Noah and Violet?" Trent lunged at Daniel with his diamond sword.

Daniel shielded himself from the blow and took out a potion, which he splashed on Trent.

"I feel so weak!" Trent cried.

Daniel laughed, but stopped when he saw Noah and Violet charging at him with their diamond swords.

"Game over!" Noah shouted at Daniel.

"No, game on!" Daniel let out another sinister laugh. This one was even louder than the last laugh. He quickly took off his diamond armor and splashed a potion of slowness on Noah and Violet and then splashed a potion of invisibility on himself. In an instant, Daniel disappeared.

14
BULL'S-EYE

"**N**oah!" Nina called out.

"Violet!" Hannah shouted.

"We're over here by the swampy water. Daniel splashed a potion of slowness on us, and we are moving very slowly," Violet replied.

"Where is Daniel?" asked Nina as she approached them.

"He used that potion of invisibility again. We have no idea where he went. He can't be far though," explained Noah.

"Here, take this." Nina offered them milk, which they both drank and regained their strength.

Bounce! Squish!

"Oh no!" Violet called out. "Look at the slimes!"

A group of green, cubed slimes with large black eyes bounced toward the group.

"There's no time to fight slimes, we have to find Daniel!" Nina advised.

A boxy slime bounced at Noah. "I don't think we have a choice. If we don't battle the slimes, we'll be destroyed."

Noah and Violet lunged at the slimes. They struck the globs with their diamond swords. The cubes broke into smaller slimes that then bounced toward Nina, Trent, and Hannah.

With their diamond swords out, the gang fought the slimes. As more slimes bounced toward them, Nina exclaimed, "How are we ever going to find Daniel?"

"Just concentrate on battling the slimes now," Noah said as he used all of his energy to destroy the slimy swamp creatures.

A bat flew overhead. Nina felt a potion splash on her back.

"Another witch spawned!" cried Hannah.

Nina had been splashed with a potion of weakness. Hannah raced to her side and handed her some milk. Hannah threw a potion on the witch and then struck her with her diamond sword.

"Hannah!" a voice called out.

Hannah couldn't see who it was. She was too busy trying to fight the evil witch that stood inches from her face, ready to throw a potion on her.

"Hannah! It's Ben!" Ben rushed toward Hannah, surprising the witch with a fatal blow. He was with Samson and Angela.

"How did you find us in the swamp?" asked Hannah.

"I saw you guys head in this direction," replied Ben.

"There's no time for small talk!" cried Noah. "Help us battle the slimes. And we still need to find Daniel."

Ben and Hannah joined the others in the battle against the never-ending slime invasion.

"No matter how many we destroy, more slimes seem to reappear!" Nina was exhausted and she wanted to find Daniel soon.

"Oh no!" Hannah cried, as two new witches spawned by the witch hut. The purple-robed swamp witches hobbled toward Hannah and Ben.

Ben struck one witch, but it drank a potion and regained its strength. Noah shot arrows at the witches.

Nina destroyed a large slime and the smaller slimes that were formed from the large slime. She was beginning to feel hopeful, when five more slimes bounced toward them.

"Where are these slimes coming from?" Nina wailed.

"I'll bet Daniel is spawning them!" cried Violet.

"Should we try and find the spawner?" asked Noah.

"I think we should just battle these slimes and witches. We can't afford to lose anyone here," Ben said as the witch threw a potion at him, and he stood frozen in the dark swamp.

The sun began to rise. The gang destroyed the slimes, but the witches remained. With a burst of determination, the group shot a barrage of arrows at the witches until they were destroyed.

"Daniel is probably miles from here by now." Nina was disappointed. She wanted him caught.

"I wouldn't bet on it," added Trent. "Daniel isn't going to lose out on the opportunity to destroy the final Olympic games."

"You're right." Nina replied. "The archery competition starts soon. I don't want Daniel ruining the event. Now that we know Mac is working for Daniel, I'm even more worried. This means Daniel knows all the details about the competition. He can really plan a serious attack."

The gang drank potions of healing to regain their strength after the nighttime swamp battle, and then ran toward Olympic Village. They had to protect the spectators and they had to ensure the archery competition was going to take place that morning.

As they reached Olympic Village, they saw people entering the archery stadium. Violet and her friends weaved through the crowd to enter. Violet examined the stadium floor to check for endermites and silverfish. She went over to the hole Daniel had filled with lava. The hole was gone! She became suspicious and wondered who had filled it in.

The spectators took their seats. A man wearing a red Olympic jacket stepped onto the stage and announced the start of the archery competition.

Violet asked Nina, "Is he really an Olympic official?"

"Yes, but as we now know, that means nothing. Mac was also an Olympic official. And Daniel has the sprinter working for him. I don't trust anyone who is involved with these Olympic games."

The man in the red jacket shot an arrow into the sky, signifying the start of the archery competition. The spectators watched in awe as the skilled athletes tried to hit the bull's-eye that hung on the stadium wall. The first athlete missed the bull's-eye, and the spectators let out a disappointed sigh.

The second athlete jumped onto the stage and aimed his arrow. He wasn't trying to strike the bull's-eye though. He aimed straight for Violet.

"Watch out!" Nina shouted to Violet as the arrow flew through the air and struck Violet's arm.

"Gotcha!" the athlete laughed.

The spectators watched in horror. They couldn't believe an athlete was shooting at a member of the audience.

Daniel leapt onto the stage and instructed his team of evil minions, "Come on guys! Attack!"

The frightened spectators rushed for the exit.

Kaboom!

An explosion rocked the ground by the stadium's exit. Dozens of spectators were destroyed.

Violet could hear Daniel's sinister laugh through the chaos. She also heard him utter, "Bull's-eye!"

15
SNEAK ATTACK

"**E**veryone, please remain calm." Nina stood in the center of Olympic Village, delivering a speech to the worried spectators. "The games will go on. Daniel, an evil griefer, is trying to destroy these games. We won't let him. Will we?"

The spectators cheered and shouted in unison, "No, we won't!"

"We need to stop Daniel!" Nina called to the crowd. "And we also have to stop the people working with him!"

One spectator, wearing an Olympic hat he had purchased at one of the kiosks filled with Olympic merchandise, called out, "How do we do that?"

Nina stood silently. The spectator was asking her to come up with a plan. Nina knew she wanted Daniel destroyed, but she wasn't sure how to accomplish it. Nina just stared at the crowd. She had no response.

Violet walked up to Nina and stood beside her. "I have a plan!" Violet announced and the crowd cheered.

"We need to capture Daniel," Violet told them. "We outnumber him, so we will win. All you have to do is follow me!"

The enormous group of spectators trailed behind Violet as she led them back into the archery stadium. Violet felt a bit overwhelmed by this power. But she believed having all of these people backing her up would ensure a victory. Or at least she hoped this was true. Violet could see Daniel sneaking to the back of the archery stadium. She raced toward him and the spectators followed.

Daniel was cornered. His hole had been closed up and he had nowhere to run; within minutes, Violet and the numerous spectators crowded the small room behind the archery arena.

"The game is over now, Daniel!" Violet shouted.

"You think your makeshift army can stop my plans. Even if you destroy me, the game isn't over, because I'm not the only one playing," Daniel laughed.

Violet aimed an arrow at Daniel and shot it. The arrow struck Daniel's unarmored chest. "Bull's-eye!" Violet called out.

"One hit isn't going to destroy me," Daniel laughed again.

Kaboom!

A large TNT explosion rocked the stadium.

The stadium exploded, destroying the spectators, Violet, and Daniel.

Violet respawned in the hotel room. She looked out the window of the room to see Olympic Village in ruins. The archery stadium was destroyed. She had led the spectators to their destruction. Violet grabbed some milk from her inventory and took a drink. She dashed out of the hotel to search for her friends and to put an end to Daniel's attacks.

"Violet!" Noah yelled.

"Were you destroyed in the stadium attack?" Violet asked.

"No, I was outside the stadium," explained Noah. "But I saw Daniel. He must have respawned close to Olympic Village."

"Where is he?" Violet asked.

The spectators rushed from the hotel and raced to Violet's side.

Violet was shocked. "I led you to your destruction. I put you in harm's way. How can you still want to follow me?"

The spectator with the Olympic hat called out, "That wasn't your fault. You were just letting us help you battle Daniel. He must be stopped. We will follow you until we destroy him."

Violet was thrilled. With all of these people helping her, there was no way Daniel could win.

The sky grew dark and rain began to fall on the crowd.

"Daniel is staging another hostile mob invasion," Violet informed them. "He's controlling this. Make sure you are armored up and ready for battle."

Violet saw Hannah, Ben, Angela, Samson, Trent, and Nina approaching her. Nina shouted, "He's summoned skeletons and zombies! We can see them heading toward Olympic Village!"

Noah looked up at the sky. "And another Ender Dragon," he said as the large dragon flew through the rainy sky and let out a loud roar.

"I hope he doesn't summon the Wither," Violet said as she shot an arrow at the flying menace.

"Too late," Nina cried. A purple light flashed through the wet grey sky and the Wither spawned.

Skeletons shot arrows. Zombies lumbered toward the crowd and struck spectators. The Ender Dragon lunged at the group, striking them with its powerful wings. The Wither shot wither skulls. They were being attacked from all angles. Violet could hear Daniel laughing as he stood by the Olympic hotel carrying bricks of TNT.

Violet raced toward Daniel, dodging blows from the hostile mobs that were invading the Olympic village.

"Don't you dare blow up that hotel!" Violet shouted. She knew if the hotel was destroyed, the group would have nowhere to respawn. She too would have no place to respawn. Violet shot an arrow at Daniel.

Noah hurried to aid Violet. He was carrying a bucket. When he got close enough, he threw the bucket at Daniel.

"Lava!" Daniel cried. He was destroyed.

Violet and Noah grabbed the bricks of TNT and placed them in their inventory. "We can't let Daniel blow up the hotel," Violet said to Noah. He agreed.

Nina jogged over to them. "I know where Daniel will respawn," she told them, and together they headed for Daniel's respawning point.

16
AWARDS

Nina led them out of the village to a small hut located in a field near the entrance to Olympic Village.

"This is Daniel's house," she informed them.

Violet entered the house and found Daniel respawning on his bed. "Maybe I should place you on Hardcore mode," Violet said as she looked at Daniel.

"You'd never do that!" Daniel retorted.

Noah and Nina rushed in and aimed arrows at Daniel.

"Shoot me. I'll only respawn in this bed. It's a waste of your arrows," Daniel laughed.

"What do you have planned?" Violet interrogated him.

"Do you think I'd tell you?" He laughed again.

"Why are you destroying the Olympics?" Violet was exasperated.

Mac walked through the door to Daniel's house and said, "Everything is set, Daniel."

"What is set?" Nina asked Mac.

"It's too late. Give up the fight," Mac told her.

"Never. And I can't believe you're working with Daniel. We worked so hard to plan these Olympic games. Why would you want to destroy them?" Nina was confused. She and Mac had spent months planning these games and recruiting athletes from around the Overworld. She wondered what Daniel was offering Mac that would make him join forces with such an evil person.

Mac looked at Nina and smiled. "Because it's fun."

"Fun?" Nina shouted and then shot an arrow at Mac.

"Why did you do that?" Mac was startled, and he lost a heart when the arrow hit his arm.

"You need to stop this, Mac. You're hurting people. It isn't fun. It's evil." Nina shot another arrow at Mac.

"Stop!" Mac shouted, "I'm not only working with Daniel because it's fun. He also promised me riches and control over parts of the Overworld."

Violet pointed her arrow at Daniel when he tried to get out of his bed. She spoke to Mac, "This man doesn't offer anyone riches. He doesn't care about you. He isn't going to give you control over anything. All he wants is control over you."

"It's true," Nina added. "Daniel won't give you control. He's just a bully."

Kaboom!

An explosion was heard in the distance.

"What did you blow up now? The hotel?" Violet was very upset; she looked at Daniel and shot an arrow at him.

"You're going to have to return to the village to find out what we destroyed," he laughed. "Leave me here!"

"No, Daniel, you're not going anywhere," stated Violet. She then asked her friends to keep an eye on Daniel and Mac. She had a plan.

Violet hurried out of Daniel's house and quickly started to craft a bedrock room.

Noah joined Violet and asked, "Do you need help?"

"Yes, I want to finish this fast. I am going to put Daniel and Mac in this bedrock prison. There's no way they can escape from here," Violet noted as she crafted the building.

"What a great idea," Noah said. He helped Violet construct the small building.

When they had finished the house, she returned to Daniel's house with Noah at her side.

"Daniel, this is over. You need to give up." She held her diamond sword close to Daniel's chest.

Daniel let out another sinister laugh. "Stop this talk, Violet. You're just wasting your time. When will you give up? Don't you want to return to Olympic Village and see what I've destroyed?"

"No!" Violet shouted.

Noah stood over Daniel with a potion of harming, while Nina aimed her arrow at Mac.

"Come with us," demanded Violet.

There was nowhere to hide. Daniel had to admit he was trapped. They marched Daniel and Mac to the bedrock house.

"This is your new home." Violet led them into the house. "And you won't be able to leave."

Daniel and Mac reluctantly entered the bedrock house. They tried to dart away right before they walked through the entrance, but Noah and Nina shot arrows at them. Once they were in the house, Nina built a bedrock wall, trapping them.

"This is where you're going to spend the rest of your time in the Overworld," Violet told them.

"We have to find out what they have done to the Olympics," said Noah.

"Is it safe to leave them here without anyone keeping watch?" asked Nina.

"I think there's no way they can get out of that bedrock room," Violet informed her friends. "We need to save the Olympics."

The trio headed for Olympic Village. The town was still in the thick of the battle with the Ender Dragon.

Violet looked up at the sky and ran over to Trent. "Where's the Wither?"

"It exploded. We destroyed it!" Trent exclaimed while he battled a zombie with his diamond sword.

Violet struck the zombie. It took a few more blows from their swords and the zombie was destroyed.

"This is a very harsh attack." Trent was exhausted. "Many people are feeling defeated. They don't want to fight anymore. They just want to leave the Olympic games."

But as he spoke, the sun began to shine and the hostile mobs disappeared.

Violet, Noah, and Nina joined the villagers and threw snowballs at the weakened Ender Dragon, destroying the fiery beast as it flew through the sky.

An End Portal emerged in the corner and people began flocking to the portal. They wanted any escape from the Olympic village. Even though the End was harsh, they knew the rules in that world. They couldn't deal with the constant surprise attacks Daniel had staged on the Olympics. Also, if they went to the End and were defeated, they'd respawn in another part of the Overworld. The spectators wanted to escape from the Olympic games, and they were willing to take chances.

Nina stood in the center of Olympic Village and announced the good news, "There's no need to travel to The End through that portal. We have captured Daniel!"

"We don't believe you!" one of the spectators called out.

"Follow us!" Violet called out.

She led the group from the Olympic village toward the bedrock house. She truly hoped Daniel would still be inside the impenetrable structure when they arrived. Even though she had constructed it and believed there was no escaping the bedrock prison, she still wondered if Daniel could escape.

17
THE REAL WINNERS

The crowd followed Violet to the bedrock house. Once they reached the house, Violet pointed out Daniel and Mac through a small window.

"Why is everyone staring at me? I'm not a caged animal. This isn't the zoo," he snapped. Daniel was very upset.

"Now that I've proven Daniel is trapped, will you promise not to leave? Please watch the final Olympic games and the closing ceremonies," Violet pleaded with the group.

The crowd cheered when they saw Daniel imprisoned. Violet was pleased, but she realized the sprinter was still on the loose. She didn't like the idea of Daniel having any minions free to terrorize the Olympics.

As they all made their way back to Olympic Village, Violet searched for the sprinter. She knew he was fast, and he could get away quickly, but she needed to find him.

"Will everyone help me rebuild the archery stadium, so we can finish up the games?" Violet asked the group.

The spectators listened to Violet as she informed them what needed to be done to rebuild the stadium. Within a couple of hours the stadium was completed.

"It looks great!" Violet declared as she surveyed the finished stadium. She was so happy that the final game could go on.

"Everyone enter the stadium, so we can declare a gold medal winner for the archery competition," an announcer declared.

The excited crowd filed in, and everyone took their seats, waiting for the athletes to enter the stage.

After several competitors took their turns, an athlete raised his bow and aimed for the bull's-eye, and with one hit, the arrow landed smack in the center.

"Bull's-eye!" the crowd called out and began to cheer.

They had a winner. Nina walked onto the stage and presented the Olympic archery champion with a gold medal skin. He wore it proudly.

"This is the end of the Olympic games! We had four gold medal winners. And we even had one from this town," Nina said proudly.

Violet looked over at Noah. She couldn't believe one of her best friends was an Olympic gold medal winner. She was happy for Noah. He smiled back at Violet.

Violet could see the sprinter in the audience. She wondered what he was planning. When the sprinter noticed Violet staring at him, he got up from his seat and left the stadium. Violet trailed behind him, and followed him outside the stadium.

"Stop!" Violet yelled at the sprinter as he ran through the Olympic village. He didn't turn around, and Violet raced after him.

"Leave me alone!" he called out to Violet as she ran closely behind him.

Violet didn't have much energy left and knew she couldn't continue that pace for much longer. Breathlessly she called to the sprinter, "Daniel is trapped. You don't have to listen to him now."

The sprinter stopped abruptly. "What?" he gasped. He was shocked.

"Yes, we trapped Daniel in a bedrock prison. He can't escape."

"What about Mac?" asked the sprinter.

"He's also trapped in the bedrock room."

"He's the one who forced me to destroy the Olympics," the sprinter confessed.

"Please, will you tell me what Daniel was planning?" asked Violet.

"Daniel wanted to destroy the closing ceremonies. He planned to blow up the entire Olympic Village. He also was hoping the explosion was powerful enough to create a hole in the ground and people would fall into lava. His ultimate goal was to transform the village into a sea of lava that could never be built on again."

"That's horrible!" Violet couldn't believe how awful Daniel's plan was and she was glad that she was able to stop it.

"I can show you where he was storing the remaining TNT," the sprinter said, and he led Violet to a large brick building outside the Olympic village. She convinced the sprinter to ignite the building.

Kaboom!

The TNT exploded, and the Olympic games were officially saved.

Violet thanked the sprinter as they made their way back to the village for the closing ceremonies.

"I'm so glad I can't be terrorized by Mac anymore," he said. The sprinter was happy to be free.

Violet entered the Olympic village and was surprised to hear cheers coming from the crowd that filled Olympic Square.

"You saved the day!" the spectators called out.

18
END GAME

"Let's begin the closing ceremonies!" Nina announced. The crowds in Olympic Square cheered.

Nina continued, "We need to thank Violet for saving the games! And for creating the stunning stadiums, some of which she had to build a few times."

"I didn't build them alone," Violet confessed. "I want to thank everyone here who helped me build the stadiums and battle Daniel. I couldn't have done it by myself. This is everybody's victory."

The crowd cheered again!

Valentino asked, "Who's hungry?"

Everyone began to gather food for a feast. Trent and the sprinter helped organize the celebration. Violet walked over to them.

"It's so nice to see you both working together for something that is fun and enjoyable and doesn't hurt anybody," Violet said with a smile.

Trent and the sprinter agreed, but Trent said, "I still feel like people are looking at me as if I'm the bad guy."

"That's not true. People accept you and all that you have done for this town. You have truly helped us."

Jack joined the group. "Most of this town used to be rainbow griefers who worked for Daniel."

"You mean this is the town that stole Daniel's griefer army?" The sprinter was shocked. "You're legendary."

"Yes, it is. I used to be a rainbow griefer, but I learned that I could make my own choices. Now I am living in this town quite happily," Jack informed them.

"I'd love to stay here and practice my running," the sprinter announced.

"I'd also love to stay," Trent added, "but I'm a treasure hunter and I'm only happy when I'm roaming the Overworld in search of treasure with my friends Max, Henry, and Lucy." Trent looked off in the distance; he imagined all of the jungle temples and water monuments he might encounter during his treasure hunting trips. He wanted to explore every inch of the Overworld, but he admitted that if he ever grew tired of traveling, this would be the town he'd settle in.

Noah walked over to Violet. "I can't believe we beat Daniel again. This one was a tough job."

"And the other battles with Daniel were easy?" Violet joked.

"No. But I hope he really stays in that bedrock house. I'd love to live in a world where we wouldn't have to worry about Ender Dragons and the Wither tormenting us," confessed Noah.

"Me too!" proclaimed Violet.

Nina joined the gang. "We need to start the parade." She looked at Noah, "You are one of our gold medalists, so you get to ride on a float."

Violet was excited to see her friend on a parade float being celebrated by the entire Olympic community.

The parade began, and Violet and the others stood watching the many floats pass by. They were especially happy when they saw the first float thatcarried Noah and the other gold medalists pass by. Noah waved to the crowd as he wore his gold medal skin.

At the end of the parade, the sun had set and the closing fireworks display began. Violet stood in awe of the colorful light show in the dark night sky. When the fireworks show ended, everyone headed to the hotel to go to sleep. Tomorrow they would journey back to their towns all across the Overworld. Violet stood in the empty Olympic Square. She loved the peaceful silence and knowing that everyone was safe.

THE END

SNEAK PREVIEW FROM

THE RETURN OF THE RAINBOW GRIEFERS

AN UNOFFICIAL LEAGUE OF GRIEFERS ADVENTURE, #4

1
GRAND OPENING

"That was fast!" Noah remarked as he stepped off the Dashing Coaster. The epic superfast roller coaster was the main attraction at the new amusement park, which opened right outside Violet and Noah's town.

"I want to ride the Ferris wheel," Violet said as she walked toward the purple Ferris wheel.

"The Ferris wheel? That's boring. I want something that goes crazy fast!" Noah loved thrill rides.

The new amusement park was called Supersonic, and people traveled from all around the Overworld to attend its grand opening. Violet was excited because she helped craft the tilt-a-whirl ride. She had also designed the food court for the amusement park. Her good friend Valentino the Butcher had a restaurant at the park, and Violet went to visit him. Valentino was serving some customers.

"Do you have a break?" asked Violet.

"Not at the moment." Valentine replied.

"We wanted to see if you'd like to ride the Dashing Coaster with us." Violet smiled.

"I think we've been on it at least ten times. I've lost track," added Noah.

"It sounds like fun, but I have to cook." Valentino frowned.

"If you find time for a break, let us know. We'd love to ride the coaster with you," replied Violet.

Violet was disappointed Valentino couldn't join them, but she was also eager to explore the rest of the amusement park with Noah. There were so many rides they hadn't tried out. All the rides used command blocks, so they got to go extremely fast and were able to have blocks teleport. Violet pointed to a ride shaped like a large pirate ship, that swayed back and forth. "Let's go on that one!"

Noah agreed, and they climbed abroad the pirate ship. When Violet was high up in the air on the pirate ship, before it made its severe dip, which made Violet's stomach feel a bit off, she saw a flash of pink in the distance. She was very quiet when she stepped off the ride.

"Didn't you like the ride?" asked Noah.

"I did. But I thought I saw something when we were on the ride. I think I must have been imagining it." Violet looked off in the distance. She didn't see anything suspicious. She hoped the pink wasn't from a rainbow griefer's skin and it was someone walking with colorful cotton candy.

"We have to go to the opening celebration event," Noah told Violet as the two walked toward the center of the amusement park. Violet agreed, and the went to the celebration.

Katie and Leo, the folks who developed the amusement park, stood on a podium and addressed the crowd.

Katie announced, "Welcome to Supersonic. We are happy to be here. This park took a lot of planning, but now that it's finished, we want you to enjoy all of the rides!"

The crowd cheered.

Leo stood in front of a water ride. "We are opening the log flume. Line up and be the first to experience this incredible ride!"

Noah and Violet walked to the front of the line. Violet loved the log flume. They sat next to each other, and they both screamed when the flume took a big dip.

"I think that was my favorite ride," remarked Violet when exiting the ride.

"There are so many more rides to go on. I don't think we can pick our favorites yet."

Violet noticed her friends Hannah and Ben walking in the distance, and called out to them.

Hannah sprinted toward them. "Violet and Noah, you have to come with us!"

Violet and Noah followed Ben and Hannah. Violet asked, "Where are we going?"

"We already went on all of the rides in this section of the park." Noah was annoyed. He wanted to explore the rest of the park.

"We're not going on a ride." Hannah tried to catch her breath.

"We saw something by the Dashing Coaster," Ben told them, "and I think it was a pink—"

Violet interrupted, "Rainbow griefer?!"

"Yes!" Hannah was upset.

"I thought I saw a pink rainbow griefer when I was on the roller coaster. I was hoping that I imagined it." Violet looked for the griefer.

"I thought we disbanded the rainbow griefer army." Ben didn't understand how they could return. All of the rainbow griefers had changed their skins and were living peacefully in Noah and Violet's village.

"And we trapped Daniel in the bedrock house. You promised us that he couldn't escape." Hannah looked at Violet for confirmation.

"We have to go to the bedrock house. We have to see if Daniel is still there." Violet sprinted to the exit.

Kaboom!

"Was that thunder?" Ben stopped and looked up at the dark sky as rain began to fall on the park.

"Zombies!" Hannah shouted.

Amusement park visitors tried to seek shelter from the rain and the zombies. Hordes of people sprinted toward the food court. Violet, Noah, Hannah, and Ben suited up in diamond armor and sprinted toward the zombies that surrounded Katie and Leo.

"Help us!" Katie called out in terror.

Noah struck a zombie with an arrow. Ben sprinted toward the zombies with his diamond sword, striking two.

A zombie attacked a villager working at cotton candy kiosk, transforming the villager into a zombie villager.

Violet used her diamond sword to destroy the zombie that attacked the villager. She gave the zombie villager a golden apple and splashed a potion to save him.

"Thanks!" The villager told Violet, as Violet rushed over to Katie and Leo.

Katie and Leo tried to fight back, but they didn't have diamond armor. A zombie struck Katie. She was losing energy. With one more hit from the undead beast, she would be destroyed.

Noah hit the zombie that stood next to Katie. "Bull's-eye!"

Violet gave Katie some milk to regain her strength.

The sun peeked through the clouds and the zombies disappeared.

"Now I am sure that was a pink rainbow griefer by the Dashing Coaster." Violet looked at the sky.

"What's a pink griefer?" asked Leo.

The gang described Daniel's griefer army and told them the story about how they helped dissolve the army.

"Why do you think this is Daniel's fault?" questioned Katie.

"I have a feeling that zombie attack was staged by Daniel. It's a typical move of his. I'm sure he wants to destroy this amusement park." Violet's mind was racing. She wanted to stop Daniel.

"Why would he want to destroy Supersonic? This is a fun place for everyone in the Overworld." Leo was confused.

"That's exactly why he would destroy it. He doesn't like to see anyone have a good time," replied Ben.

"When our village hosted the Olympics, Daniel caused all sorts of trouble. The only way we could stop him was by trapping Daniel in a bedrock house. We need to see if he's still there. I usually go by and check, but I have been so busy working on the amusement park." Violet had many excuses for not visiting Daniel. She disliked traveling outside of town and having to check on him.

"Lead us to Daniel," Katie demanded. "We need to stop him before he stages any more attacks on Supersonic."

But it was too late. The gang could hear someone from the Fun House shout, "Lava!"

People rushed out of the Fun House, as the group ran toward them.

"What happened?" Violet called to the people who stood outside the Fun House.

"Someone flooded the Fun House with lava," a man in a red hat called out.

Leo tried to create order in the chaotic environment. He told everyone to stay calm and move away from the house. People were still racing out of the Fun House as a pool of lava oozed out from the front door.

Leo screamed, "Stand back!"

Violet looked at the grassy meadow outside the amusement park, Daniel's bedrock makeshift prison lay just beyond the bucolic landscape. She took a deep breath before embarking on their journey toward the bedrock home. She wasn't sure what she'd find when she got there.

DO YOU LIKE FICTION FOR MINECRAFTERS?

Check out other unofficial Minecrafter adventures from Sky Pony Press!

Invasion of the Overworld
MARK CHEVERTON

Battle for the Nether
MARK CHEVERTON

Confronting the Dragon
MARK CHEVERTON

Trouble in Zombie-town
MARK CHEVERTON

The Quest for the Diamond Sword
WINTER MORGAN

The Mystery of the Griefer's Mark
WINTER MORGAN

The Endermen Invasion
WINTER MORGAN

Treasure Hunters in Trouble
WINTER MORGAN

Available wherever books are sold!

LIKE OUR BOOKS FOR MINECRAFTERS?

Then check out other novels by Sky Pony Press.

Pack of Dorks
BETH VRABEL

Boys Camp: Zack's Story
CAMERON DOKEY, CRAIG ORBACK

Boys Camp: Nate's Story
KITSON JAZYNKA, CRAIG ORBACK

Letters from an Alien Schoolboy
R. L. ASQUITH

Just a Drop of Water .
KERRY O'MALLEY CERRA

Future Flash
KITA HELMETAG MURDOCK

Sky Run
ALEX SHEARER

Mr. Big
CAROL AND MATT DEMBICKI

Available wherever books are sold!